Anson D. F Randolph

Hopefully Waiting and Other Verses

Anson D. F Randolph

Hopefully Waiting and Other Verses

ISBN/EAN: 9783337090685

Printed in Europe, USA, Canada, Australia, Japan

Cover: Foto ©Andreas Hilbeck / pixelio.de

More available books at **www.hansebooks.com**

HOPEFULLY WAITING,

AND

OTHER VERSES.

BY

ANSON D. F. RANDOLPH.

NEW YORK:

CHARLES SCRIBNER AND COMPANY,

654 BROADWAY.

1867.

RIVERSIDE, CAMBRIDGE:
STEREOTYPED AND PRINTED BY
H. O. HOUGHTON AND COMPANY.

I desire that the Public should know, *my dear* SCRIBNER, *that this little volume has been made at your request ; and that but for you I would have been content with such circulation as these verses have already had in the newspapers and magazines of our country.*

A. D. F. R.

NEW YORK, September, 1866

CONTENTS.

	PAGE
HOPEFULLY WAITING	7
BRIDGES	10
RICH, THOUGH POOR	13
TO ——	16
EARTH TO EARTH	17
LITTLE BESSIE	20
THE CANARY BIRD	24
FAR OFF, YET NEAR	25
BY FAITH AND PATIENCE	27
TO F——	28
SONG	29
SABBATH MORNING	31
HAPPIEST DAYS	33
THE NEW GIFT	36
LOSS AND GAIN	37
GOOD-NIGHT	39
THE MASTER'S INVITATION	40

Contents.

	PAGE
THE STORY OF MARGARET BROWN	43
LESS AND MORE	48
FAIRY TALES	50
THE COLOR-SERGEANT	55
"THE MARRIED STATE IS A STATE OF SORROW"	59
TO F. F. R.	62
LITTLE LUCY, AND THE SONG SHE SUNG	65
THE ABSENT LORD	68
HYMN FOR THE DEDICATION OF A CHURCH	71
SOJOURNING, AS AT AN INN	73
OUR BABY	76
THE WILD FLOWER	79
SONG	80
THE LOVING MASTER	82
THE HAPPY PILGRIM	83
A HOUSEHOLD LAMENTATION	85
A SUNBEAM AND A SHADOW	88
NO ROOM FOR HIM	90
MASTER, IS IT I?	93
TRUST ABSOLUTE	94
LONGINGS	97
"THAT PASSETH UNDERSTANDING"	99

POEMS.

———

HOPEFULLY WAITING.

" Blessed are they that are Homesick, for they shall come at
last to the Father's House." — HEINRICH STILLING.

NOT as you meant, O learnèd man and good,
    Do I accept thy words of hope and rest;
God knowing all, knows what for me is best,
And gives me what I need, not what he could,
      Nor always as I would !
I shall go to the Father's House and see
    Him and the Elder Brother face to face,
What day or hour I know not. Let me be
    Steadfast in work, and earnest in the race,

Not as a homesick child, who all day long
Whines at its play, and seldom speaks in song.

If for a time some loved one goes away,
    And leaves us our appointed work to do,
    Can we to him or to ourselves be true,
In mourning his departure day by day,
        And so our work delay?
Nay, if we love and honor, we shall make
    The absence brief by doing well our task,
Not for ourselves, but for the dear one's sake;
    And at his coming only of him ask
Approval of the work, which most was done,
Not for ourselves, but our belovèd one!

Our Father's House, I know, is broad and grand;
    In it how many, many mansions are!
    And far beyond the light of sun or star,
Four little ones of mine through that fair land
        Are walking hand in hand!
Think you I love not, or that I forget
    These of my loins? Still this world is fair,

And I am singing while my eyes are wet
  With weeping in this balmy summer air ;
Yet I 'm not homesick, and the children *here*
Have need of me, and so my way is clear !

I would be joyful as my days go by,
    Counting God's mercies to me. He who bore
    Life's heaviest cross is mine for evermore ;
And I, who wait his coming, shall not I
        On his sure word rely ?
So if sometimes the way be rough, and sleep
  Be heavy for the grief he sends to me,
Or at my waking I would only weep,
  Let me be mindful that these things must be,
To work his blessèd will until he come,
And take my hand and lead me safely home.

BRIDGES.

A BRIDGE within my heart,
    Known as the " Bridge of Sighs,"
That stretches from life's sunny part
    To where its darkness lies.

And when upon this bridge I stand,
    To watch the tides below,
How spread the shadows on the land, —
    How dark the waters grow !

Then as they wind their way along
    To sorrow's bitter sea,
How mournful is the spirit-song
    That upward floats to me.

A song that breathes of blessings dead,
    Of joys no longer known,

And pleasures gone, — their distant tread
  Now to an echo grown.

And hearing thus, beleaguering fears
  Soon shut the present out ;
The good but in the past appears,
  The future full of doubt.

Oh, often then doth deeper grow
  The night that round me lies ;
I would that life had run its flow,
  Or never found its rise.

II.

A BRIDGE within my heart,
  Known as the Bridge of Faith ;
It spans by a mysterious art
  The streams of life and death.

And when upon this bridge I stand,
  To watch the tides below,
How glorious looks the sunny land, —
  How clear the waters flow !

Then as they wind their way along
   And to a distant sea,
I listen to the angel-song
   That sweetly floats to me.

A song of blessings never sere,
   Of love beyond compare ;
And life so vexed and troublous here,
   So calm and perfect there.

And hearing thus, a peace divine
   Soon shuts each sorrow out,
And all is hopeful and benign,
   Where all was fear and doubt.

Oh, ever then will brighter grow
   The light that round me lies ;
I see from life's beclouded flow
   A crystal stream arise !

RICH, THOUGH POOR.

NO rood of land in all the earth,
   No ships upon the sea,
Nor treasures rare of gold or gems
   Do any keep for me:
As yesterday I wrought for bread,
   So must I toil to-day;
Yet some are not so rich as I,
   Nor I so poor as they.

On yonder tree the sunlight falls,
   The robin 's on the bough;
Still I can hear a merrier note
   Than he is warbling now:
He 's but an Arab of the sky,
   And never lingers long;
But this o'erruns the livelong year
   With music and with song.

Come, gather round me, merry ones,
    And here as I sit down,
With shouts of laughter on me place
    A mimic regal crown.
Say, childless King, would I accept
    Your armies and domain,
Or e'en your crown, and never feel
    These little hands again?

There 's more of honor in their touch,
    And blessing unto me,
Than kingdom unto kingdom joined,
    Or navies on the sea:
So greater gifts by them are brought
    Than Sheba's Queen did bring
To him who at Jerusalem
    Was born to be a king.

Look at my crown and then at yours,
    Look in my heart and thine;
How do our jewels now compare, —
    The earthly and divine?

Hold up your diamonds to the light,
   Emerald and amethyst ;
They 're nothing to these love-lit eyes,
   Those lips so often kissed !

" O noblest Roman of them all ! "
   That mother good and wise,
Who pointed to her little ones,
   The jewels of her eyes :
Four sparkle in my own to-day,
   Two deck a sinless brow ;
How grow my riches at the thought
   Of those in glory now !

And still no rood of all the earth,   ·
   No ships upon the sea,
No treasures rare of gold or gems
   Are safely kept for me :
Yet I am rich — myself a king !
   And here is my domain ;
Which only God shall take away
   To give me back again !

TO ——.

NAY, not so, dearest! Look into my eyes,
  Giving the search its clearest, amplest range;
Look in my heart, and see if there arise
  In all its palpitations, new or strange,
One pulse of doubt, or smallest sign of change!
We have come hence the common road along,
And ours the common lot; for we have seen
Some lights go out, and darkness fill the way,
And even then, our hearts so full of song,
Sang to each other, as we passed between
The storm and cloud-drifts of the waiting day.
Think you such love could its dear object wrong?
I have thy answer as I give thee mine;
Yet all I can bestow, how mean compared with
    thine.

EARTH TO EARTH.

HERE are flowers, dead and gone,
   All their sweetness is withdrawn;
Look upon these faded leaves,
Whereunto no beauty cleaves;
Look upon these withered stems,
They have lost their gold and gems;
Back to thee, O Earth, I give
What for me no more doth live.

Other flowers of mine thou hast,
Upon which a death hath passed;
Sweeter flowers than these were they,
But their life has sped away,
And for them a bed was made
By the sexton's busy spade;
Back to thee, O Earth, I gave
What I could not spare or save!

2

Still rich flowers thou hast of mine,
And not long shall they be thine;
Sweetest sweets are soonest gone,
What is best is first withdrawn;
In the sunlight, in the shade,
Some will sicken, some shall fade;
One by one I shall receive,
Caring not how much you grieve.

This, O Earth! thy voice to me,
Softly saith and mournfully,
While my heart is sore with pain,
Sitting with the dead again;
While a mist is in my eyes,
And the night about me lies;
Now thy voice of solemn tone
Speaketh of thy realm alone,

While a better Voice I hear,
Falling from another sphere;
Earth! thou shalt not always keep
These of mine that with thee sleep;

What I give thee back to-day,
Keep, and welcome, keep for aye;
But the others are not thine,
They are God's, and will be mine,
When upon thy pulseless breast
I shall lay me down to rest.

LITTLE BESSIE,

AND THE WAY IN WHICH SHE FELL ASLEEP.

HUG me closer, closer, Mother,
    Put your arms around me tight;
I am cold and tired, Mother,
    And I feel so strange to-night!
Something hurts me here, dear Mother,
    Like a stone upon my breast:
Oh, I wonder, wonder, Mother,
    Why it is I cannot rest.

All the day, while you were working,
    As I lay upon my bed,
I was trying to be patient,
    And to think of what you said, —
How the kind and blessed Jesus
    Loves his lambs to watch and keep,

And I wished he 'd come and take me
  In his arms, that I might sleep.

Just before the lamp was lighted,
  Just before the children came,
While the room was very quiet,
  I heard some one call my name.
All at once the window opened :
  In a field were lambs and sheep ;
Some from out a brook were drinking,
  Some were lying fast asleep.

But I could not see the Saviour,
  Though I strained my eyes to see ;
And I wondered, if he saw me,
  Would he speak to such as me ;
In a moment I was looking
  On a world so bright and fair,
Which was full of little children,
  And they seemed so happy there.

They were singing, oh how sweetly !
  Sweeter songs I never heard ;

They were singing sweeter, Mother,
　　Than our little yellow bird;
And while I my breath was holding,
　　ONE, so bright, upon me smiled,
And I knew it must be Jesus,
　　When he said, "Come here, my child.

"Come up here, my little Bessie,
　　Come up here and live with me,
Where the children never suffer,
　　But are happier than you see;"
Then I thought of all you 'd told me
　　Of that bright and happy land;
I was going when you called me,
　　When you came and kissed my hand.

And at first I felt so sorry
　　You had called me; I would go;
Oh to sleep, and never suffer; —
　　Mother, don't be crying so!
Hug me closer, closer, Mother,
　　Put your arms around me tight;

Oh how much I love you, Mother;
  And I feel so strange to-night!

And the mother pressed her closer
  To her overburdened breast;
On the heart so near to breaking
  Lay the heart so near its rest;
At the solemn hour of midnight,
  In the darkness calm and deep,
Lying on her Mother's bosom,
  Little Bessie fell asleep!

THE CANARY BIRD.

BLITHELY thy morning song breaks on my ear
    Here in the city's dust, O gentle bird;
And now the dank o'ercrowded atmosphere,
The ceaseless noise that everywhere is heard,
Is lightened by thy music. While it springs
A wish for woods and fields where flowers be,
It drops into my heart from viewless wings
Something far better than their fragrancy.
Thou art a patient, life-long prisoner,
Shut from the world, and in thy solitude
Sighing for freedom, yet the almoner
To me of song with cheerfulness imbued;
I listen, and my restless heart grows calm,
And I with thee lift up contentment's psalm.

FAR OFF, YET NEAR.

O BLESSED Lord!
   Once more, as at the opening of the day,
 I read thy Word;
And now, in all I read, I hear thee say,
" To those who love I will be ever near; "
And yet while this I hear,
To me, O Lord, thou seemest far away.

   Thou Sovereign One,
Greater than mightiest kings, can it be fear,
   Or blinding sun
Made by thy glory, so if thou art here,
I cannot see thee; yet this Word declares
That whoso loves, and bears
Thy Holy Name, shall have thee ever near!

I bear thy name;
That love, dear Lord, have I not long confessed?
   Thy love 's the same
As when, like John, I leaned upon thy breast,
And knew I loved; oh, which of us has changed?
Am I from thee estranged?
O Lord, thou changest not: I know the rest!

   My doubting heart
Trembles with its own weakness, and afraid
   I dwell apart
From thee, on whom alone my hope is stayed:
I would, and yet I do not know thy will
And perfect love; am still
Trusting myself, to be by self betrayed.

   O blessed Lord!
Far off, yet near, on me new grace bestow,
   As on thy Word
I go to meet thee; even now, I know
Thou nearer art than when my quest began;
One cry, and thy feet ran
To meet me; Lord, I will not let thee go!

BY FAITH AND PATIENCE.

KEEP on sowing:
    God will cause the seeds to grow
Faster than your knowing;
Nothing e'er is sown in vain,
    If, his voice obeying,
You look upward for the rain,
    And falter not in praying.

    Keep on praying:
In the brightest, darkest day,
    Still his voice obeying;
Never from the gates of prayer
    Turn with doubting sorrow,
For the One who standeth there
    May answer you to-morrow!

TO F——.

NO poet e'er hath sung a song to her,
    No painter from her radiant features stole
Glimpses of beauty, such as fill the soul
And captive hold the dreamy worshiper.
The gay saloon hath never been astir
At her incoming presence. She doth pass
Unnoticed through the world, save by the few —
Such as make search for flowers amid the grass,
In shaded nooks half hidden from the view.
Known only as a patient wife and true,
She rules with quiet grace her small domain;
She homage hath the queenliest never knew,
And is content each duty to pursue,
That crowns with daily blessings all her reign.

SONG.

THE flowers which blessed the early Spring,
 And crowned the Summer hours,
Lie dead along the mountain slope,
 Or in their valley bowers;
So blessings on the Autumn sun,
 That nursed these buds for me:
I bring them straight to thee, my love;
 I give them all to thee!

The morning air was clear and warm,
 The evening's damp and chill,
And some who oft are good and kind
 To-day have served me ill;
So blessings on the steadfast heart
 That knows no change to me:
I find the sunlight here, my love,
 I left at morn with thee.

What if these buds shall ne'er unfold,
　　Soon perish like the flowers ;
Their fragrance evermore shall float
　　About this home of ours ;
So blessings on the heart that turns
　　All things to joy for me :
The World may have its way, my love,
　　When I come back to thee !

SABBATH MORNING.

O DAY of love and calm delight,
    " The brightest of the seven ";
O precious foretaste of the rest
    And blessedness of heaven.

The birds have sung since morning broke
    And yonder moon grew dim;
They never had so sweet a voice,
    Or sang a sweeter hymn.

The river that at yester eve
    Dashed wildly on the shore,
Moves calmly downward to the sea,
    That vexes it no more.

Where'er I turn to hill or plain,
    Above me or around,

A quiet fills the outward world,
  Like that within me found.

O blessed scene of peace and love,
  That seems to heaven akin,
Is this a world of pain and death,
  Of sorrow and of sin?

Shall the sweet birds forget their song,
  And tempests sweep the river?
This blissful scene, my quiet heart,
  Remain unchanged forever?

The coming eve may bring the wind,
  The early morn the rain,
And backward send the noisy world,
  To fill my heart again!

Come night of wind, or morn of rain,
  Or changes sad to see;
If, Lord, thou art my Refuge still,
  Why should they trouble me?

HAPPIEST DAYS.

THEY tell us, Love, that you and I
    Our happiest days are seeing,
While yet is shut from either's eye
    The changes of our being.
Ah! life they say 's a weary way,
    With less of joy than sorrow, —
That where the sunlight falls to-day,
    There 'll be a shade to-morrow.

If ours be love that will not bear
    The test of change and sorrow,
And only deeper channels wear
    In passing to each morrow,
Then better were it that to-day
    We fervently were praying,
That all we have might pass away
    While we the words were saying.

3

The heart has depths of bitterness,
    As well as depths of pleasure,
And those who love, love not unless
    They both of these can measure;
There is a time — 't will surely come --
    When each this must discover,
And woe if either then be dumb
    To that which moved the lover.

There are some spots where each will fall,
    Where each will need sustaining;
And suffering is the lot of all,
    And is of God's ordaining.
Then wherefore do our hearts unite
    In bonds that none can sever,
If not to bless each changing light,
    And strengthen each endeavor?

Then while these happy days we bless,
    Let us no doubt be sowing;
God's mercy never will be less,
    Though he should change the showing.

Such be our faith, as on we tread,
    Each trusting and obeying,
As two who by his hand are led,
    And hear what he is saying.

THE NEW GIFT.

TWO years ago our gracious God
    To us a child did give, —
A darling one now gone from us,
    With Christ the Lord to live.

That gift, it opened in our hearts
    A spring unknown before ;
And death — it sealed the fountain up,
    To open here no more.

Now when our God, whose name be praised,
    Another child has given,
Whose sunny face we often think
    Is like a face in heaven,

We say that she can never fill
    The place so filled before ;
While wondering why our loss should seem
    To make us love her more !

LOSS AND GAIN.

HOW sadly beats the heavy autumn rain;
     How mournful drives the wind among the
          trees;
Along the shore the weary sailor sees
The waves roll in that send him out again;
The birds are restless in the scattered leaves;
The clouds move wildly each in massy fold,
And all the outer world, or earth, or air,
But yesterday so warm, so fair,
Is changed, and in a night, to drear and cold.

Now goes the golden autumn far away,
Now nearer comes the winter to my door;
And thus does Nature, working evermore,
Create new life from changes and decay.
O Christ! who in the hall of Pilate bore

For me the scourge and mocking ; for thy sake
Fill up the daily loss in life of mine
With thy life. So shall love divine
Out of the changing the unchanging make.

GOOD-NIGHT.

GOOD-NIGHT ! a sweet voice laughing said ;
  And by the hope within me born,
I knew we only said good-night
  To meet again at morn.

Good-night ! one time it softly said ;
  And by the heavy heart I bore,
I knew full well we said Good-night, —
  Good-night, for evermore

Ah, sweet it was to say Good-night,
  When morning could our joys restore ;
What grief to part beneath the stars,
  And meet on earth no more !

THE MASTER'S INVITATION.

DEAR Lord, thy table is outspread;
    What other could such feast afford?
And thou art waiting at the head,
    But I am all unworthy, Lord;
        Yet do I hear thee say, —
          (Was ever love so free?)
        Come hither, son, to-day,
          And sit and sup with me.

O Master! I am full of doubt,
    My heart with sin and fear defiled;
Come thou, and cast the tempter out,
    And make me as a little child;
        Methinks I hear thee say, —
          Come thou, at once, and see
        What love can take away,
          And what confer on thee.

My Lord! to thee I fain would go,
  Yet tarry now I know not why;
Speak, if to tell what well I know,
  That none are half so vile as I.
    What do I hear thee say? —
      Look, trembling one, and see
      These tokens, which to-day
      Tell what I did for thee.

Nay, Lord! I could not here forget
  What thou didst for my ransom give;
The garden prayer, the bloody sweat,
  All this and more, that I might live.
    I hear thee sadly say, —
      If this remembered be,
      Why linger thus to-day?
      Why doubt and question me?

Oh, love to angels all unknown!
  I turn from sin and self aside;
Thou hast the idol self o'erthrown,
  I only see the CRUCIFIED;

I only hear thee say, —
A feast is spread for thee
On this and every day,
If thou but follow me!

MARGARET BROWN.

I.

HARD by the brook, beyond the town,
   Where stands the leafless locust-tree,
There is a cottage, old and brown,
Which rearward looks upon the town,
   But faces to the sea.

The walks with grass are overgrown,
   And weeds fill up the garden-bed ;
The moss clings to the stepping-stone,
And from the tree the birds have flown,
   Now that the tree is dead.

Mid all these dreary signs without,
   And scarce a sound of life within,

The passer stops and looks about,
As half in fear and half in doubt
    Of what may here have been.

Ah, 't is a simple tale and rare
    Of life the stranger cannot know, —
There is a presence in the air,
As if of angels watching there,
    Or passing to and fro.

Here Margaret lives, " Old Margaret Brown," —
    Thus doth the clerk her name record, —
With what is given by the town ;
Nor notes what daily is sent down
    In blessings from the Lord.

Here she was born and here was wed,
    Here grew her children by her side,
Till one by one from her they fled, —
And there they laid her husband dead,
    Brought shoreward by the tide.

Thus blessings came, thus from her went, —
  God's love by sun and shadow shown ;
You say a heart so torn and rent,
With all its loving forces spent,
  Might harden into stone ?

Ah, years did follow, all unblessed, —
  How bleak was all the world, — how dark !
Her wandering soul, in search of rest,
Only the gloom and waste possessed,
  Nor found the only ark !

Oh, faithless soul that would not know,
  Who ever watched or went before ;
And sought in all those waves of woe,
In all their flood and overflow,
  To give thee peace once more.

II.

Oh, happy day, but all too brief,
  And night more precious still than day ,

When she obtained the dear relief,
That left her still the sense of grief,
　　But stole the sting away !

She sat in silence with her dead,
　　When Jesus came and called her name ;
One answering word, and fear and dread
Went out, and unto her, instead,
　　A holy quiet came.

Oh change that did her soul astound ;
　　The Lord had come and talked with her,
And all her grief with comfort crowned ;
She had once more the Master found,
　　Beside the sepulchre.

Long years have passed — poor, blind, and old,
　　She waits until God's will is done ;
And yet her closèd eyes behold
That world of glories manifold,
　　And Jesus as the sun.

What if the sea roar up the beach,
  The leafless tree the sound prolong;
Her soul its resting-place can reach,
Still tune the common words of speech
  Into a thankful song.

What if the stone no more be pressed
  By steps that woke a welcome sound;
Her loving heart is full of rest, —
With her abides a heavenly guest, —
  The Lord whom she has found.

And if the birds have spread the wing,
  The walk with grass be overgrown;
She seems to hear the downward ring
Of songs, such as the angels sing,
  Where sorrow is unknown!

O world, with all thy pomp and pride,
  So poor, so full of doubt and fear;
Lo, Christ, with gifts to thee denied,
Has every longing satisfied,
  And built his temple here!

LESS AND MORE.

TWO prayers, dear Lord, in one —
    Give me both less and more:
Less of th' impatient world, and more of thee;
    Less of myself, and all that heretofore
Made me to slip where ready feet do run,
    And held me back from where I fain would
        be, —
    Kept me, my Lord, from thee!

All things which most I need
    Are thine: thou wilt bestow
Both strength and shield and be my willing Guest;
    Yet my weak heart takes up a broken reed,
Thy rod and staff doth readily forego,
    And I, who might be rich, am poor, distressed,
    And seek but have not rest.

How long, O Lord, how long?
  So have I cried of late,
As though I knew not what I well do know:
  Come thou, Great Master Builder, and create
Anew that which is thine; undo my wrong —
  Breathe on this waste, and life and health be-
      stow :
  Come, Lord, let it be so!

Let it be so, and then —
  What then? My soul shall wait,
And ever pray — all prayers, dear Lord in one —
  Thy will o'er mine in all this mortal state
Hold regal sway. To thy commands, Amen!
  Break from my waiting lips till work is done,
  And crown and glory won!

4

FAIRY TALES.*

THE picture of a little child
  That comes to us from o'er the sea :
Why hath it thus my heart beguiled, —
  Why such a charm for me ?

Before it oft I stop and gaze,
  And pass the rarer pictures by,
Until the shopman, in amaze,
  Would seem to ask me why.

He does not know, nor need I tell,
  Where, in that face, a look I see

* A picture by a foreign artist of a little child, seated and reading a large book.

Of one, who for a while did dwell
   On earth to comfort me.

The picture of a little child, —
   A book, a child, and nothing more ;
And she to quiet reconciled
   By Fairy Tales of yore.

What joy, what wonder on her face,
   And such as children only know ;
And Art has caught each changeful grace,
   And will not let it go.

O childish face ! thou art not mute,
   Thou giv'st my thought mysterious range ;
Here in thy presence I compute
   A story sweet and strange ;

The story of a little life,
   So brief, and yet withal so sweet ;
'T would seem a dream, but for the strife
   That made the life complete.

Thus many a time in days gone by,
    A child, who dwells with us no more,
(How deep the shadows now that lie
    Where sunlight was before,)

Would sit, a book within her hand,
    Her eye intent upon the page,
As though she well did understand
    What did her sight engage.

O blessed child! I see thee still!
    My heart o'erleaps the solemn years,
And eyes thou once with light didst fill,
    Thou fillest now with tears.

And yet through Sorrow's cloud and mist
    My eager sight is swift to run
Through sapphire hues, and amethyst,
    And glory of the Sun;

Until thy face, with wondrous change,
    I, as in vision, clearly see;

O child of mine, O marvel strange!
  What might I learn of thee!

Two score of years, what have they brought
  Of knowledge to compare with thine?
The narrow reach of human thought,
  To that which is divine!

The mysteries of our mortal state,
  At which I shrink as they unfold;
Nor fear nor wonder can create
  In them who God behold!

Sweet child, not mine as heretofore,
  Still mine in glory yet to be;
Dear Lord, could I desire more
  Concerning her of thee?

O throbbing heart! thy longings cease,
  Come, patient Lord, thy grace bestow,
And turn this sorrow into peace,
  That shall more perfect grow.

This picture of a little child,
By one who dwells across the sea,
Thus hath it oft my heart beguiled,
And been a joy to me!

THE COLOR-SERGEANT.

YOU say that in every battle
    No soldier was braver than he,
As, aloft in the roar and the rattle
    He carried the Flag of the Free?
I knew, ah! I knew he'd ne'er falter,
    I could trust him, the dutiful boy;
My Robert was willful, — but Walter,
    Dear Walter, was ever a joy.

And if he was true to his mother,
    Do you think he his trust would betray
And give up his place to another,
    Or turn from the danger away?
He knew while afar he was straying,
    He felt in the thick of the fight,
That at home his poor mother was praying
    For him and the cause of the Right!

Tell me, comrade, who saw him when dying,
  What he said, what he did, if you can ;
On the field in his agony lying,
  Did he suffer and die like a man ?
Do you think he once wished he had never
  Borne arms for the Right and the True ?
Nay, he shouted, " Our country forever ! "
  When he died he was praying for you !

O my darling ! my youngest and fairest,
  Whom I gathered so close to my breast ;
I called thee my dearest and rarest,
  And thou wert my purest and best !
I tell you, O friend ! as a mother,
  Whose full heart is breaking to-day,
The Infinite Father — none other —
  Can know what He 's taken away.

I thank you once more for your kindness, —
  For this lock of his bright auburn hair ; —
Perhaps 't is the one I in blindness
  Last touched, as we parted just there !

When he asked, through his tears, should he linger
  From duty, I answered him, Nay;
And he smiled, as he placed on my finger
  The ring I am wearing to-day.

I watched him leap into that meadow :
  There a child he with others had played ;
I saw him pass slowly the shadow
  Of the trees where his father was laid ;
And there, where the road meets two others,
  Without turning he went on his way ;
Once his face toward the foe, not his mother's
  Should unman him, or cause him delay.

It may be that some day your duty
  Will carry you that way again,
When the field shall be riper in beauty,
  Enriched by the blood of the slain :
Would you see if the grasses are growing
  On the grave of my boy ? Will you see
If a flower, e'en the smallest, is blowing,
  And pluck it, and send it to me ?

Don't think, in my grief, I 'm complaining ;
    I gave him, God took him, — 't is right ;
And the cry of his mother remaining
    Shall strengthen his comrades in fight.
Not for vengeance, to-day, in my weeping,
    Goes my prayer to the Infinite Throne ;
God pity the foe when he 's reaping
    The harvest of what he has sown !

Tell his comrades these words of his mother :
    All over the wide land to-day
The Rachels, who weep with each other,
    Together in agony pray.
They know, in their great tribulation,
    By the blood of their children outpoured,
We shall smite down the foes of the Nation
    In the terrible day of the Lord.

"THE MARRIED STATE IS A STATE OF SORROW."

D EAR heart, what say you, is the proverb true,
  This German proverb of the olden time?
Or did some cynic, who had wed a shrew,
Attempt the act to rue,
  By ringing out this simple, solemn rhyme:
    Live by thyself, all will be well;
    Who wed shall weep to-morrow;
    And find too late that married state
    Is state of pain and sorrow.

It is not true! — how ready to deny
  This well-kept wisdom of five hundred years;
How dare you now to make such curt reply, —
With laughter to deny
  That which to some most doleful truth appears.

Nay, nay, you trifle ! 'T is no idle jest;
　　This is a proverb — do you heed it so ?
And proverbs, they by some men are confessed
Of simple truths the best;
　　Come read it o'er again, and clear and slow.

Still doubting and denying, and with speech
　　That 's less conclusive than that look of thine :
Art thou by silence seeking to impeach
The cynic ; by its reach
　　Take in our life, and say, *not true of mine !*

'T is I that trifle ?　Tell me how you know !
　　Ah, well you prove it — give me then your hand :
Do you remember now the years ago,
And when I held it so,
　　While God's own servant forged the endless
　　　　band ?

And now your face, some say, is not so fair
　　As on that morning of our marriage day ;
And yester eve, the children in my hair

Searched out the silver there,
And laughed to think that I was growing gray.

Wellnigh a score of years have gone their round
   Since we passed out to journey side by side;
And say, dear heart, have we not always found,
Where faith and love abound,
   What else is needed will not be denied?

God's benediction was upon the rite,
   And God's dear mercies followed with the deed;
So e'en in days of darkness, when the night
Was over long, and light
   Came slowly, we said not, whate'er our need,
      Live by thyself, all will be well;
      Who wed shall weep to-morrow;
      And find too late that married state
      Is state of pain and sorrow.

TO F. F. R.

TO-NIGHT, where gleam the stars benign
    Above the broad Catalpa-tree,
O friend, I pledge thee in this wine, —
    The wine thou gavest me.

More generous, sunlight and the dew
    And winds that feed the autumn rain
Ne'er nursed in vineyards, old or new,
    That crowd the slopes of Spain.

The peasant throng with shout and dance
    This vintage gathered years ago :
Nor dreamed what guest and circumstance
    Should quaff or mark its flow.

It may have been at feast, where song
    And dance disturbed the fragrant air;

While noisy guests sat late and long,
　To pledge the bridal pair.

Perhaps where met the proud and great,
　Their studied praises to bestow,
On one who well had served the state
　In its convulsive throe.

At kingly boards it may have passed,
　Where nobles sat with monarchs crowned ;
When fulsome words the lie surpassed
　In which the toast was drowned.

So too in homes, on festive days, —
　Those days that household joys restore,
Perchance has graced life's common phrase
　When turned to Love's once more.

With pledge at feast of bridal pair,
　At board of statesman, home, or king,
I place as pledge beyond compare,
　That which I give and bring.

Not such as flattering lips bestow, —
　The idle word betricked with art:
He honors most, as true men know,
　Who honors with the heart!

And shall not I, O friend, to thee
　For unrecorded deeds of thine
Give thanks, as now I hold and see
　Thy gifts to me and mine?

And so, where gleam the stars benign
　Above the broad Catalpa-tree,
I pledge again, but not in wine, —
　HE WHO IS FRIEND TO ME!

LITTLE LUCY, AND THE SONG SHE SUNG.

I.

A LITTLE child, six summers old, —
    So thoughtful and so fair,
There seemed about her pleasant ways
    A more than childish air, —
Was sitting on a summer eve
    Beneath a spreading tree,
Intent upon an ancient book
    That lay upon her knee.

She turned each page with careful hand,
    And strained her sight to see,
Until the drowsy shadows slept
    Upon the grassy lea ;
Then closed the book, and upward looked,
    And straight began to sing

5

A simple verse of hopeful love —
   This very childish thing :
" While here below, how sweet to know
   His wondrous love and story ;
And then, through grace, to see his face,
   And live with him in glory ! "

II.

That little child, one dreary night
   Of winter wind and storm,
Was tossing on a weary couch
   Her weak and wasted form ;
And in her pain, and in its pause,
   But clasped her hands in prayer —
(Strange that we had no thoughts of heaven
   While hers were only there) —

Until she said : " O mother dear,
   How sad you seem to be !
Have you forgotten that he said
   ' Let children come to me ' ?
Dear mother, bring the blessed Book, —
   Come, mother, let us sing."

And then again, with faltering tongue,
　She sung that childish thing:
" While here below, how sweet to know
　His wondrous love and story;
And then, through grace, to see his face,
　And live with him in glory!"

III.

Underneath a spreading tree
　A narrow mound is seen,
Which first was covered by the snow,
　Then blossomed into green;
Here first I heard that childish voice
　That sings on earth no more;
In heaven it hath a richer tone,
　And sweeter than before:
" For those who know his love below " —
　So runs the wondrous story —
" In heaven, through grace, shall see his face
　And dwell with him in glory!"

MY Lord was taken from me: day by day
   My heart grew sadder with the sins it bore,
While many dulcet voices came to say,
   Why weepest thou?   If he come back no more,
Give o'er thy sorrow, needless at the best.
   So I their call obeyed,
   And knew not, yet would know where he was
      laid,
   And could not be at rest.

I was a wanderer thence from place to place;
   I questioned some who sat within the gate,
And saw the play of the incredulous face;
   On others scanned the look of scorn and hate.
My heart grew hard, — I say not how or why, —
   While oft my search was stayed;

And then I cared not where my Master laid,
  Or would his name deny.

Thus in the day I could my loss forget,
  Or he was crowded from me by the press;
At night, my soul with many fears beset,
  Would oft with tears its shame and loss confess,
    And sick, alone, afraid,
  Cry out, O world, tell where my Lord is laid,
    Or let me love thee less.

One time I thought on Peter in the hall,
  And soon of Mary waiting at the grave;
Then of the smiting of the threat'ning Saul, —
  And was not Jesus near to help and save?
O light that came, and why the long delay?
  I had my Lord conveyed
  Afar, forgetting where he had been laid,
    And gone upon my way.

My way, and he had risen to follow me, —
  Me all unworthy, ne'er by him forgot;

O wondrous love, that could so patient be !
  My eyes were holden that I knew him not !
Peace came at last, as to the twain that day
  Who from Jerusalem strayed ;
    And while they talked of where he had been laid,
      He met them by the way !

HYMN FOR THE DEDICATION OF A CHURCH.

IN every place, O Sovereign Lord,
  On ocean, plain, and mountain-side,
Thy Name, for man, thou dost record,
  The promise with him to abide.

Where mortal eye hath never seen,
  Where foot of man hath never trod,
Thy kingly messengers have been,
  And left the impress of their God.

Here, Lord, thy grander work begin,
  Where thy dear love recorded stands ;
Come now, and take, and enter in
  This temple built by willing hands.

Thy name record, thy grace unfold ;
  Here dwell this day, and evermore ;
Let us, and those to come, behold
  Thy glory, and as ne'er before.

We plead thy promise free and great ;
  Accept the gift, and make it thine :
O Holy Ghost, for thee we wait
  To make our human work divine !

SOJOURNING, AS AT AN INN.

I LOOK abroad upon the verdant fields,
   The song of birds is on the summer air;
Within, how many a treasure something yields,
   To bless my life and round the edge of care;
     And yet the earth and air,
     All that seems good and fair,
That still is mine or for a time hath been,
Now teach me I am but a pilgrim here,
   Without a home, and dwelling at an inn.

Not always has the outlook been so clear:
   There have been days when stormy gusts went
      by, —
Nights when my wearied heart was full of fear,
   And God seemed farther off than stars and sky;
     Yet then, when grief was nigh,
     My soul could sometimes cry

Out of the depths of sorrow and of sin,
That at the worst I was but pilgrim here,
   With home beyond, while dwelling at an inn.

Now I complain not of this life of mine,
   I less of shade have had than of the sun;
The gracious Father, with a hand divine,
   Has crowned with mercies his unworthy one;
         My cup has overrun,
         And I, his will undone,
   Have changed his countless blessings into sin,
As I forgot I was but pilgrim here,
   Homeless at best, and dwelling at an inn.

Look on me, Lord! Have I not need to pray
   That this fair world, that gives so much to me,
Serve not to lead my steps so far astray
   That at the end I stand afar from thee?
         Dear Lord, let this not be;
         Nay, rather let me see
   Beyond this life my happiest days begin;

And singing on my way, a pilgrim here,
   Rejoice that I am dwelling at an inn.

Dear Son of God ! by whom the world was made,
   Yet homeless — had not where to lay thy head,
(Not e'en by kindred was thy body laid
   In Joseph's tomb, thou Lord of quick and dead !)
      By thy example led,
      Of me may it be said,
When I shall rest and perfect peace begin,
He lived as one who was a pilgrim here,
   And found his home while dwelling at an inn.

OUR BABY.

O F all the darling children
　　That e'er a household blessed,
We place our baby for compare
　With the fairest and the best;
She came when last the violets
　Dropped from the hand of Spring;
When on the trees the blossoms hung —
Those cups of odorous incense swung —
　When dainty robins sing.

How glowed the early morning
　After a night of rain,
When she possessed our waiting hearts
　To go not out again;

" Dear Lord," we said, with thankful speech,
  " Grant we may love thee more
For this new blessing in a cup
  That was so full before ! "

SEPTEMBER, 1858.

II.

This year, before the violets
  Had heralded the Spring,
And not a leaf was on the trees,
  Nor robin here to sing,
An angel came one solemn night,
  Heaven's glory to bestow,
And take our darling from our sight :
What could we, Lord, at morning light,
  But weep, and let her go !

How dark the day that followed
  That dreary night of pain ;
Those eyes now closed, and never more
  To open here again !

" Dear Lord," we said, with broken speech,
 " Grant we may love thee more
For this new jewel in the crown
 Where we had *two* before!"

SEPTEMBER, 1860.

THE WILD FLOWER.

IT grew upon a sloping bank,
  Beside a common stone;
There in the starry silence drank
  The dews of heaven alone.

Uncared for, and by some unseen,
  It lived serenely there,
To grace one little spot of green,
  And bless the common air.

The idle dreamer passing by
  No gladness from it caught;
It could not fill his restless eye,
  Or waken pleasant thought.

So may I pass my humble lot,
  Content to be unknown,
If thus from me some hidden spot
  A touch of sweetness own.

SONG.

I KNOW where by life's wayside
   There is a crystal spring,
Where sometimes I sit down and sigh,
   But oftener sit and sing;
None tarry there so long as I,
   Or there so frequent be,
For it for none does outward flow
   As it flows out to me.

In th' dryest days of Summer
   The current sweeps along,
And Winter brings no ice to freeze
   The measure of its song;
So, like a good thought of the soul,
   That wanders out to bless,
It every day but deeper grows,
   Instead of growing less!

Ask you where by life's wayside,
  On what enchanted ground,
This crystal spring, so sweet, so rare,
  Is ever to be found?
Look down into your heart, my love,
  As I into your eyes,
And while I trace the outward flow,
  You may behold the rise.

6

THE LOVING MASTER.

*A*ND *the same night in which he was betrayed,*
    (So runs the record of that Feast of thine,)
While the Eleven joyous, yet afraid,
    Scarce knew the meaning of the bread and wine,
And on the Other heavy guilt was laid,
    Nor fear nor knowledge touched thy love divine.
What if thy coming death the hour oppressed,
    No human grief should on the service wait,
    Or guilt of one then sadden or abate
The grace and peace that served the loyal guest.
Dear, patient Lord, if at thy Table here
    I sit unworthy, let not this withhold
Thy Love from any : unto all appear,
    O Christ, as to thy faithful ones of old!

THE HAPPY PILGRIM.

I.

A PILGRIM with his lot content,
  Not seeking rest below,
Now to the land that lies beyond
  With steadfast heart I go.
O foolish world, I ask no more
  Thy willing guest to be;
Mine is the rich and heavenly feast,
  And Jesus sups with me.

II.

Full often where I take my way
  Are pastures green and fair,
And living waters, cool and sweet,
  Which all the pilgrims share.
Oh, never has the day seemed long,
  The night proved drear or cold,

So that I heard his loving voice,
  Or rested in the fold !

III.

You wonder at the songs I sing,
  That so my face should shine ;
Remember, friends, that I am His,
  And He forever mine :
So I a pilgrim through the world
  A princely portion share,
While He makes every burden light,
  Or doth the burden bear !

IV.

Come then, and as a pilgrim gain
  A bliss unknown before ;
Though crowded is the way and strait,
  There still is room for more :
What if the way be rough to-day,
  The night prove drear or cold,
It shall not change his loving voice,
  Or shut us from the fold !

A HOUSEHOLD LAMENTATION.

ROOM, Mother Earth, upon thy breast for this
    young child of ours ;
Give her a quiet resting-place among thy buds and
    flowers ;
Oh, take her gently from our arms unto thy silent
    fold,
For she is calmly beautiful, and scarcely two years
    old,
And ever since she breathed on us hath tender
    nursing known :
No wonder that with aching hearts we leave her
    here alone.

How we shall miss the roguish glee, the ever merry
    voice,
That in the darkest, dreariest day would make us
    to rejoice !

How sweet was every morning kiss, each parting
    for the night,
Her lisping words, that on us fell as gently as the
    light !
But Death came softly to the spot where she was
    wont to rest,
And bade us take her from our home and lay her
    on thy breast.

So, Mother, thou hast one child more, and we a
    darling less ;
One sunny spot in all our hearts seems now a
    wilderness,
From which the warm light of the Spring has wan-
    dered swift and far,
And nothing there of radiance left but Memory's
    solemn star ;
We gaze a moment on its light, then sadly turn
    aside,
As though we now had none to love, and all with
    her had died.

Mother, we know we should rejoice that she has
    gone before —

Gone where the withering hand of Death shall never
    touch her more,

Up to the clime of sinless souls, a golden harp to
    bear,

And join the everlasting song of singing children
    there ;

Yet, when we think how dear she was to us in
    her brief stay,

We can but weep that one so sweet so early passed
    away.

A SUNBEAM AND A SHADOW.

I.

I HEAR a shout of merriment,
   A laughing boy I see;
Two little feet the carpet press,
   And bring the child to me.

II.

Two little arms are round my neck,
   Two feet upon my knee;
How fall the kisses on my cheek!
   How sweet they are to me!

III.

That merry shout no more I hear,
   No laughing child I see;
No little arms are round my neck,
   Or feet upon my knee.

IV.

No kisses drop upon my cheek, —
 Those lips are sealed to me ;
Dear Lord, how could I give him up
 To any but to thee ?

NO ROOM FOR HIM.

THE children heard me read again the story
    Of our dear Lord's coming to the earth ;
How he gave up his home of heavenly glory,
    To bear the sorrows of our mortal birth, —
Came, too, in manner so unknown, so lowly,
    Of parentage to poverty akin,
That no one seemed to think that he was holy,
    No room waiting for him at the inn.

They could not comprehend this strange rejection,
    This ignorance of him who came to save ;
And wondered why the Star, with sure direction,
    Knowledge only to the Wise Men gave :
When all the world for want of him was dying, —
    Even little children full of sin ; —
Their only Saviour with the cattle lying,
    No one saying, Come into the inn !

Ah, I could see their young hearts fondly turning
  Toward the Christ rejected by the Jews:
Heavenly Master, all of life discerning,
  Shall these ever thy dear love refuse?
They might have known, said they, *that it was Jesus,*
  And the way they treated him a sin;
And, Father, don't you think that God, who sees us,
  Knows we would have told him to come in?

Out of the mouths of babes, O Sovereign Teacher,
  Thou dost praise to thy great name ordain;
The child unto the Father comes as preacher,
  And the message makes the duty plain:
The young heart at the manger overfloweth,
  Counts thy treatment by the Jews as sin;
Nor dreams that one who all thy suffering knoweth,
  Ever said he would not let thee in.

Thou Son of Mary, when at Bethlehem lying,
  Few there were thy kingly nature knew;
And the wretched world, thy name denying,
  Pierced thy soul with sorrows through and
    through.

No wonder that the ignorant, unbelieving,
　Mocked alike thy coming and thy kin ;
Oh marvel now that one thy grace receiving
　Hath no room, or fails to ask thee in !

No room for thee, though knowing all thy story,
　From manger-bed to cross on Calvary ;
Content with darkness that shuts out the glory,
　They behold who watch and dwell with thee ;
Sleep, little children, who to-night have taught me
　More than learned preacher of my sin ;
For lo ! the risen Christ again has sought me,
　Hath come back, and I have let him in !

MASTER, IS IT I?

MY Master, at that board I sat to-day,
 Whereon the riches of thy love are spread, —
The blood-red wine, the white and broken
 bread, —
To feast thy poor disciples by the way.
And as I sat with very many there,
 Methought I heard thy voice unto me say,
As unto those who at Jerusalem were,
 There is among you one who shall betray!
When first I heard, I thanked thee I was clear
 Of such intent; but soon my depth of sin,
My lack of love, and weakness did appear,
 To show what faithless follower I had been;
And filled with fear I cried, as now I cry,
Have mercy, Master: Master, is it I?

TRUST ABSOLUTE.

PAUSE, O my soul, and here thy life review!
   God honors not such service, poor and mean;
Shalt thou to all the world be steadfast, true,
   And in thy sorrows only on him lean?
Thou canst not wander thus, as suits thy will,
   And have thy way, and cold and selfish be, —
Denying thus his name, while claiming still
   His gracious help, when so it pleases thee:
             Nay, not so;
If thou thy Lord wouldst know,
   No more his right dispute;
   Be thy trust absolute
If daily thou in grace and truth wouldst grow.

Tell me, O soul, as here I question thee,
   If now thy gains count equal to the loss?

Look o'er the world: Ah, has it brought to thee
  From mine or mart that which outweighs the
    cross? —
His cross, and he thy Lord, as Lord of all,
  Whose great heart o'er thee yearns, while even
    here
These words of sweetest pity on thee fall, —
  My perfect love can cast out every fear.
         Even so;
And thou this love mayst know,
  This wondrous gain compute;
  Be thy trust absolute,
And evermore in grace and knowledge grow.

Call'st thou the service hard — the recompense
  Of th' reward unworthy? Not of old
So seemed it to thee. Know ye not from whence
  This change and loss? Only thyself behold!
Ye sought out other masters than thy Lord,
  And would have other loves though losing him,
Unconscious of thy loss and his reward:
  Ah, who can follow when the eyes are dim!
        Was 't not so?

Thy Lord how could ye know
   When thou wast blind and mute?
   Be thy trust absolute
If daily thou in grace and truth wouldst grow!

Comes there not now a vision of long ago?
   Thou art as Jacob wrestling at the day;
Let not the angel silent from thee go, —
   Send thou the world, and not the Lord, away!
Lovest thou me, and more than these? Such word
   He spake to Peter. Answer as did he
Out of the depths, — *Thou knowest all things,*
     Lord —
   That with my better self I do love thee!
      Loving so,
Hence let me always know
   Thy will, my own be mute;
   And with trust absolute,
By thy dear help in grace and knowledge grow!

LONGINGS.

WEARY, Lord, of struggling here
    With this constant doubt and fear,
Burdened by the pains I bear,
And the trials I must share, —
Help me, Lord, again to flee
To the rest that 's found in thee.

Weakened by this wayward will
Which controls, yet cheats me still;
Seeking something undefined
With an earnest, darkened mind, —
Help me, Lord, again to flee
To the light that breaks from thee.

Fettered by this earthly scope
In the reach and aim of hope,

Fixing thought in narrow bound
Where no living truth is found, —
Help me, Lord, again to flee
To the hope that 's fixed in thee.

Fettered, burdened, wearied, weak,
Lord, thy grace again I seek;
Turn, oh turn me not away, —
Help me, Lord, to watch and pray,
That I never more may flee
From the rest that 's found in thee.

"THAT PASSETH UNDERSTANDING."

O THOU eternal and all-sovereign One,
   By whom the worlds with all they hold were
      made, —
The Father's well-belovéd, and the Son,
   To whom coequal honor shall be paid!
One word of thine, and e'en the mightiest hills
   Would shake and fall, the ocean cease its roar,
And all that comforts or with pleasure fills
   The heart of man, be seen and felt no more!
      How can I comprehend
      That thou wilt be my friend?
I know, O Lord, that I have need of thee, —
But what am I that thou art wanting me?

The stars that bless the highway of the night,
   The sun, whose steady glory fills the day,

And hosts of angels, constant in their flight,
　With all material things thy will obey.
Of these not one in all their courses fail, —
　They ever for thy service on thee wait ;
While all combinéd powers could not prevail
　To shake thy kingdom, which alone is great :
　　Lord, can I comprehend
　　That thou shouldst be my friend ?
I know, O Lord, that I have need of thee, —
But what am I that thou art wanting me ?

I am as but the balance dust — a mote
　Which floats upon the early morning air,
That e'en a mortal king would fail to note,
　Or brush aside without a thought or care, —
A passing ripple on the sandy shore,
　That rolls and breaks, but has no power to
　　stay, —
Or, at my best, one who might be no more,
　With few to miss him in the common way :
　　How can I comprehend
　　That thou wilt be my friend ?

I know, O Lord, that I have need of thee, —
But what am I that thou art wanting me?

O Lord, I thank thee that thou hast revealed
  Such love, and honor put on one so mean ;
Thy grace the hidden mystery hath unsealed,
  I, all unworthy, have thy glory seen !
And yet the wonder grows no less that I
  May call thee Master, and thy dear name bear ;
Or that thou, Lord, for such as me shouldst die,
  And ever have me in thy loving care :
      I cannot comprehend,
      Yet know thou art my friend,
As that I evermore have need of thee, —
But what am I that thou art wanting me?

THE END.

www.ingramcontent.com/pod-product-compliance
Lightning Source LLC
Chambersburg PA
CBHW032155010726
47493CB00008BA/2706